Bharatanatyam in Ballet Shoes

words by
Mahak Jain

pictures by
Anu Chouhan

annick
press
toronto · berkeley

Cover art by Anu Chouhan, designed by Paul Covello
Interior designed by Paul Covello
Edited by Claire Caldwell

Annick Press Ltd.

We acknowledge the support of the Canada Council for the Arts and the
Ontario Arts Council, and the participation of the Government of Canada/la
participation du gouvernement du Canada for our publishing activities.

Canada

ONTARIO ARTS COUNCIL
CONSEIL DES ARTS DE L'ONTARIO
an Ontario government agency
un organisme du gouvernement de l'Ontario

Library and Archives Canada Cataloguing in Publication

Title: Bharatanatyam in ballet shoes / words by Mahak Jain ; pictures by Anu Chouhan.
Names: Jain, Mahak, author. | Chouhan, Anu, illustrator.
Identifiers: Canadiana (print) 20210330392 | Canadiana (ebook) 20210330406 | ISBN 9781773216157
  (hardcover) | ISBN 9781773216164 (HTML) | ISBN 9781773216171 (PDF)
Classification: LCC PS8619.A36854 B53 2022 | DDC jC813/.6—dc23

Published in the U.S.A. by Annick Press (U.S.) Ltd.
Distributed in Canada by University of Toronto Press.
Distributed in the U.S.A. by Publishers Group West.

Printed in Canada

annickpress.com
mahakjain.com
anumation.ca

Also available as an e-book. Please visit annickpress.com/ebooks for more details.

This book is dedicated to the hereditary
dancers of the South Asian subcontinent.

—M.J. & A.C.

Paro was excited to learn a new dance, but on the first day of ballet class, she was worried.

"What if I'm terrible?"

"You won't be," Paro's mother said. "You come from a dancing family."

"But we don't dance ballet. It's not the same."

Paro peeked inside. Dancers were twirling and swirling like little fairies. Her tippy-toes started tingling. Her toes weren't nervous!

Paro watched two dancers
show off their moves.

Marco said he learned ballet as a
baby. He could already pirouette.

"My mother taught me."

Dana said she never learned ballet.
She could helicopter, though.

"I learned by watching
breakdancing videos."

Paro's mother was a dancer too, and Paro hadn't learned ballet either.

She showed Marco and Dana what she could do.

She walked, like a Bharatanatyam dancer.

Marco and Dana were confused.

"What's the dance move?"

"I think she was walking."

Paro's face burned. She wanted to show she could dance, but they thought all she could do was walk.

Dana tried to walk like Paro. "I feel like a supermodel!"

Marco walked too. "We're supermodel dancers! Supermodel with us, Paro!"

Paro's smile returned. Dana and Marco wanted her to join!
They walk-danced in circles around the room.

"Anna Pavlova is my favorite dancer," Marco said.

"My mom likes to eat pavlova," Dana said.

"You can't eat Pavlova!"

Dana giggled. "It's my mom's favorite dessert."

"My favorite dancer is Rukmini Devi," Paro said.

"Who's that?" Marco said.

"Can you eat it?" Dana said.

Paro blushed and shook her head. She wanted to show she knew dancers too, but Dana and Marco had never heard of Bharatanatyam dancers.

Dana sniffed her tutu.
"I wish I was a dessert."

"You are. You are Dana Doughnut,
and I'm Marco Marshmallow.
We're the dessert dancers!"

Dana spun like a doughnut,
and Marco wiggled like a
marshmallow.

"Paro, what are you?"

"A pudding," she said, because her worries were puddling all around her.

There was so much about dance she didn't know.

Madame taught them how to lift their arms.

Dana mimicked Madame easily, and Marco was a pro.
But when Paro tried, she moved like a Bharatanatyam
dancer, drawn to the ground.

"What's wrong?" Madame asked.

Paro stared at the floor.
How could she explain?

She wanted to show Madame
she could dance ballet, but
Bharatanatyam kept getting in
the way.

Paro's friends tried to help.
Marco gave her books to read.
Dana sent her videos to watch.

"Just practice," they said.

Paro knew what she had to do.

"No more Bharatanatyam
practice," she told her mother.
"Only ballet."

But even when Paro and her mother danced
side by side, Paro felt she was dancing alone.

She saw how different Bharatanatyam and ballet were.
Bharatanatyam turned Paro's mother into a queen, but
a ballet dancer needed to be like a fairy.

And Paro couldn't be both. Not ever.

The next class, Paro's mother didn't stay to watch.

Paro chewed her lip in worry. Was her mother upset with her?

As Paro warmed up, she snuck glances at the door.
But her mother was gone.

Madame clapped loudly.
"Dancers, gather around," she said.

Paro glanced one last time at the
door—and her mouth dropped.

Paro's mother was marching straight to Madame—
in Bharatanatyam dress and makeup!

Paro ducked behind the other dancers.

Her mother WAS upset.

Madame pressed a button on the stereo, and classical Indian music filled the room.

Paro's mother lifted her foot. The bells on her ankles clinked and chimed.

Her eyes, lined with kohl, flared. In Bharatanatyam, even the eyes danced.

Paro's mother bent her knees. The pleats of her saree fanned open.

Paro held her breath.

She loved to watch her mother dance but not today. Bharatanatyam didn't belong in ballet class!

Then Paro's mother did something very strange.

She gave her anklets to Madame.

Madame pointed her feet.
A familiar tinkling sound filled the room.

Madame flared her eyes and slammed
a foot—just like Paro's mother.

Paro was confused.
Was Madame dancing Bharatanatyam?

And then Paro's mother did something Paro had *never* seen her mother do before.

She perked up her toes—and pirouetted. Just like a ballet dancer!

The dancers leaped to their feet.

Marco was twisting his eyes, trying to make them dance. Dana was tap-tap-tapping her foot.

A dancer at the front asked if she could touch her mother's dress. Another dancer tried to swirl her hands.

They needed more teachers!

Paro dashed forward to help.

"Do it slowly," she said to Marco. She
squinted and flashed her eyes to show him.

"You have to use your heels," she told Dana.
She taught her how to stomp and pound.

Paro watched her friends.
She couldn't believe it.

With her help, her friends became Bharatanatyam
dancers. She knew a lot about dance after all!

Paro froze. Did this mean . . .

Could she dance
Bharatanatyam in a tutu?

Paro picked her favorite ballet
position and . . . flared her eyes.

She pointed her feet and . . .
slammed the floor with a foot.

She bent her knees
into a plié and . . . hey!
This one was the same!

Paro was right. She wasn't a ballet fairy.
And she definitely wasn't a Bharatanatyam queen.

Which left only one thing . . .

Paro Janaki Shankar was a fairy queen!

Behind the Scenes

I was inspired to write a story about ballet and Bharatanatyam because of the true story of Rukmini Devi Arundale (Paro's favorite dancer) and Anna Pavlova (Marco's favorite dancer).

Rukmini Devi Arundale was born in 1904 in South India. On a visit to London at the age of twenty-one, she watched the Russian ballet dancer Anna Pavlova perform onstage. Rukmini Devi was in awe. She also wanted to be a dancer, but she had few options in her home country.

At the time, India was under the rule of the British. The British didn't approve of Indian dances performed by temple dancers, including an earlier form of Bharatanatyam. Temple dances had been practiced in India for centuries, but under British rule, the dance forms fell out of favor, even among Indians. Hereditary dancers, who had practiced and protected the dance forms across generations, were not allowed and were sometimes punished for practicing temple dances. Rukmini Devi wasn't a hereditary dancer and decided to look outward.

In 1928, Rukmini Devi found herself on the same cruise ship as Anna Pavlova and her dance company. Finally, she had a chance to learn ballet! She trained with Anna Pavlova's dance company, and she returned to India inspired: she decided to study and restore the temple dance sadir as Bharatanatyam. (Sadly, hereditary dancers still weren't allowed to perform the original temple dances.) As she toured, Bharatanatyam gained the respect of audiences, and in 1936, she founded the popular Bharatanatyam dance school Kalakshetra.

Rukmini Devi was not the only one influenced by a dance from outside her country: Anna Pavlova was too. In 1923, Anna Pavlova watched a performance choreographed by North Indian dancer Uday Shankar in London. She loved it so much she asked him to choreograph two Indian-inspired compositions for her ballet performances. He even danced alongside her!

Through dance, Rukmini Devi Arundale and Anna Pavlova reached across borders and inspired each other—uplifting dance as an art form along the way. The dance culture we have today continues to be influenced by the examples set by Rukmini Devi Arundale and Anna Pavlova. Bharatanatyam dancer Menaka Thakkar, for example, began introducing Bharatanatyam to ballet students at the National Ballet School of Canada in the 1980s!

So whether you are a ballet dancer or a Bharatanatyam dancer or a breakdancer or a ballroom dancer, only one thing matters: just dance.

Mahak

What's in a Name

No one knows for sure the origin of the name Bharatanatyam (bhaa-rut-naat-yum), but some scholars think it's a mashup of four words: bhava, raga, tala, and natya (pronounced bhaav, raag, taal, and naat-yuh). Bhava, raga, and tala refer to expression, music, and rhythm. The opening sounds of each of these words (bha, ra, ta) come together to form "Bharata," which is also how some people refer to India. In Sanskrit, an ancient Indian language still spoken today, the word "natya" means dance. Put it all together and you get Bharatanatyam: expression, music, rhythm, and dance!

Most people think of ballet (bal-ay) as French, but the dance form originated in Italy in the sixteenth century. Its name comes from the Italian word "ballare" (bahl-laa-ray), which means to dance. Initially, the dance was performed in Italian court for royals and nobles. When an Italian noblewoman named Catherine de Medici married the king of France, she introduced the Italian dance to French courts. Within a century, it became hugely popular and started to be performed on stage. Ballet as we know it today is centered around storytelling and emerged in France in the eighteenth century.

Make Some Sound

The anklets that Paro's mother wears when dancing are known as ghungroo (ghoong-roo). Ghungroo are both jewelry and musical instruments, an essential part of the dancer's movements. With every step and stomp, as dancers sweep across the stage, audiences can hear the chimes. In different parts of India, the bells are known by different names, including salangai, chilanka, aankukal, and many others.

You can make simple versions of the two types of ghungroo at home. The first is similar to a rope woven with bells, while the second is lines of bells sewn into cloth. Some dancers perform with more than two hundred bells in each ghungroo!

Ghungroo on String

- yarn
- 20 jingle bells (2.5 centimeters or 1 inch)
- scissors

1. Wrap the yarn around your ankle at least twice comfortably. Cut it to length.

2. String the yarn through about 10 bells. (You can use more if your bells are smaller in size.)

3. Repeat the process for a second ghungroo.

4. Tie the yarn around each ankle like a shoelace, separate the bells, and get dancing! To store your ghungroo, tie loosely at the ends before putting away.

Ghungroo on Cloth

- 2 felt sheets, about 8 x 20 centimeters (3 x 8 inches)
- Velcro
- 20 jingle bells (2.5 centimeters or 1 inch)
- scissors
- hot glue gun

1. Wrap the felt around each ankle, overlapping about an inch, then cut to this length.

2. Cut a strip of Velcro and stick it to the short edge of the felt. (If your Velcro isn't sticky, use the glue gun with the help of an adult.)

3. On the same side as the Velcro, put glue the size of a small fingernail directly on the felt with the help of an adult. Press a bell into the glue, and repeat the process with the remaining bells. Let cool for 5 minutes. (You can use more bells if your bells are smaller in size.)

4. Repeat the process for a second ghungroo.

5. Wrap the ghungroo around your ankles and test out your dance moves!

For a traditional look, choose white yarn or red felt and brass-colored bells—or be as colorful as you want. If you want to have even more fun, include bells of different sizes!